I have a dream that my four litt

day live in a nation where they will not be judged by the color of their skin but by… their character.

—Civil rights activist Dr. Martin Luther King, Jr., August 1963

CIVIL RIGHTS

The Movement

Civil rights activists wanted equal treatment for African Americans. They wanted to overturn the laws that allowed African Americans and other groups to be treated poorly because of their race. This difficult struggle lasted many years.

Civil Rights: The Movement describes the key events in the U.S. Civil Rights Movement of the 1950s and 1960s. It also looks at the people who bravely stood up for equality and justice.

CONTENTS

We Shall Overcome!

Civil rights activists worked for years to end discrimination against African Americans. Their progress was slow. Racism ran deep, especially in the South. Many states enforced Jim Crow laws. These laws discriminated against African Americans. Civil rights activists worked tirelessly. There was too much at stake to quit.

The protests for racial equality became known as the Civil Rights Movement. Several key organizations contributed to this movement. So did leaders such as Martin Luther King, Jr, and Malcom X. They inspired courage and hope in the African American community.

Ordinary citizens also helped to keep the movement alive. During marches and protests, many activists were **abused**. Still they continued to believe that they would "overcome." Their struggle made the entire nation take notice.

Dr. Martin Luther King, Jr., delivered his "I have a dream" speech at the March on Washington (left).

Civil Rights Time Line

April 9, 1865	The Civil War ends. U.S. President Abraham Lincoln frees all slaves.
April 9, 1866	The *Civil Rights Act of 1866* is passed, protecting the rights of former slaves.
February 3, 1870	The 15th Amendment to the Constitution is officially approved.
March 1, 1875	The *Civil Rights Act of 1875* is passed to stop discrimination in public places.
1883	The U.S. Supreme Court rules against the *Civil Rights Act of 1875.*
May 18, 1896	In *Plessy v. Ferguson*, the U.S. Supreme Court rules that "separate but equal" services do not violate the Constitution.
1909	The National Association for the Advancement of Colored Peoples (NAACP) is formed.
June 21, 1915	The Supreme Court outlaws "grandfather clauses" in *Guinn v. United States.*
June 25, 1941	The Fair Employment Practices Commission is set up.
1942	The first chapter of the Congress of Racial Equality (CORE) forms.
July 26, 1948	President Harry Truman orders an end to segregation in the military.
1954	The *Brown v. Board of Education* case ends legal separation of African Americans and whites in public schools.
December 1, 1955	Rosa Parks refuses to give up her seat on a Montgomery bus. Her arrest sparks the Montgomery Bus Boycott.
September 1957	Federal troops are sent to protect African American students in Little Rock, Arkansas.
August 28, 1963	About 250,000 people attend the March on Washington.
July 2, 1964	The *Civil Rights Act of 1964* is signed into law.
August 6, 1965	The *Voting Act of 1965* is signed. The act outlaws unfair voting practices.
April 4, 1968	Dr. Martin Luther King, Jr., is shot and killed in Memphis, Tennessee.

abused
treated cruelly

Equal Education

1951–1957

Oliver Brown tried to enroll his daughter in a local school in Topeka, Kansas, in 1951. The "whites-only" school turned her away because she was African American. The nearest school for African American children was farther away. Brown asked the NAACP for help. The NAACP was already campaigning against segregated public schools. It decided the time was right to launch a big challenge.

NAACP lawyer Thurgood Marshall argued that "separate but equal" schools and other places went against the Constitution. He said that segregation also allowed people to treat African Americans unfairly. Marshall took the case to the U.S. Supreme Court. He combined Brown's case with the cases of nearly 200 other people from five states. The case was called *Brown v. Board of Education of Topeka, Kansas*. In 1954, the Supreme Court declared segregated public schools illegal.

People lined up outside the U.S. Supreme Court in December 1953 (below). They wanted to hear NAACP lawyers argue against segregation in public schools.

Federal troops protect the Little Rock Nine as they enter the front door of Central High School in Little Rock, Arkansas.

"**We conclude that, in the field of public education, the [idea] of 'separate but equal' has no place. Separate educational facilities are [by nature] unequal.**"

—*U.S. Supreme Court Chief Justice Warren in the case of* Brown v. Board of Education, *May 17, 1954*

CASE STUDY

Little Rock Nine

On September 4, 1957, nine African American students (right) arrived at Central High School in Little Rock, Arkansas. When they reached the door, soldiers turned them away at the order of Governor Orval Faubus. The nine students, now known as the Little Rock Nine, tried for three weeks to enter the school. They were met with violent protests from white students.

On September 24, President Eisenhower announced that he would send federal troops to protect the African American students. For the rest of the school year, the Little Rock Nine suffered great abuse. The lone senior had to be guarded at graduation. The events in Little Rock showed Americans how strong racism was in some parts of the nation. It also showed what a small group of people could accomplish with courage and determination.

Freedom Riders

1961

By 1961, some states were still allowing segregation and separate services for African Americans. Members of the Congress of Racial Equality (CORE) wanted to draw attention to the situation. They were inspired by nonviolent protests. They sent a group of volunteers on a bus trip through parts of the South. They were called the Freedom Riders. They tried to use **facilities** in bus stations along the way.

On May 14, a Freedom Rider bus was surrounded by a violent mob in Anniston, Alabama. The Freedom Riders were beaten as they left the bus. The **incident** appeared on the front page of newspapers across the nation. Soon after the attack in Anniston, another mob attacked the Freedom Riders in Birmingham, Alabama. The Freedom Riders feared for their lives and ended the journey.

Another group of Freedom Riders tried again. They continued the Freedom Rides from Tennessee. Alabama's governor provided police protection for the group. However, when the group arrived in Birmingham, Alabama, the police were gone. The riders were attacked by another mob.

During the next four months, several hundred Freedom Riders rode buses through parts of the South. In November, the federal Interstate Commerce Commission issued tough new rules preventing segregation on buses or trains, or in bus or train stations.

The Freedom Riders were made up of both white and African American members of CORE. The Freedom Riders on the left are preparing to go to Washington to demand federal protection of African American civil rights.

facilities
places that are set up for particular purposes

incident
one event that may form part of another larger event

In Anniston, white mobs blocked buses carrying Freedom Riders (left). Some of the mob then slashed the tires on the bus and set fire to it. The passengers were attacked as they fled the bus.

CASE STUDY

Congress of Racial Equality

James Farmer (right), a civil rights activist founded the Congress of Racial Equality (CORE) when he was only 22 years old. The organization's first actions were sit-ins. Their purpose was to get service for African Americans in Chicago restaurants. The plan was successful and was later copied by other civil rights activists. Farmer and CORE also helped others organize successful protests, including the Montgomery Bus Boycott, the March on Washington, and the Freedom Riders. CORE continues to fight inequality today.

I Have a Dream...

1963

The *Brown v. Board of Education* decision came in 1954. It was a major victory for the Civil Rights Movement. Segregation didn't end, though. A young activist, Dr. Martin Luther King, Jr., wanted to change the nation. He dreamed of a better place for all Americans. He focused on peaceful ways of ending segregation. King led the successful boycott of buses in Montgomery. Afterward, he received death threats. However, threats were not enough to stop King.

King organized marches, boycotts, and sit-ins. In 1963, King led a peaceful protest in Birmingham, Alabama. The governor of Alabama ordered police to break up the protestors. King was sent to jail.

From his jail cell in Birmingham, King wrote a famous letter. He said that all people had a duty to speak out against unjust laws, wherever they occurred. He wrote, "Injustice anywhere is a threat to justice everywhere." King's nonviolent protests worked. They soon attracted national attention and support.

King was arrested many times during nonviolent protests. He is shown here seated in a Florida jail cell with fellow civil rights activist Ralph Abernathy (left). The two men were arrested in June 1964 while peacefully protesting against segregated restaurants.

Despite their peaceful demonstrations, hundreds of protesters were arrested and jailed during King's Birmingham campaign.

> **"We have waited more than 340 years for our constitutional and God-given rights."**
>
> *—Dr. Martin Luther King, Jr., in "Letter from Birmingham Jail," April 16, 1963*

CASE STUDY

The March on Washington

On August 28, 1963, about 250,000 people joined King and other civil rights leaders to march to Washington, D.C. (right). A quarter of the marchers were white Americans. Dr. Martin Luther King, Jr., called it the "greatest demonstration of freedom in the history of our nation." King hoped the march would encourage the government to pass a new civil rights bill.

During the March on Washington, King delivered his famous "I have a dream" speech. Many consider it to be one of the best speeches in American history. People cried and hugged each other as he spoke. His powerful words about equality and freedom inspired many Americans of all backgrounds.

Civil Rights Acts

1957–1964

President Dwight Eisenhower introduced the *Civil Rights Act of 1957*. The purpose of this act was to make it easier for African Americans in the South to vote. The act was the first of its kind in 82 years. It was unpopular with some political leaders from the South. Still, the **bill** was passed by Congress and became law. Unfortunately, the act did little to stop some Southern states. They continued to discriminate against African Americans and keep them from voting.

President John F. Kennedy entered office in 1961, and he publicly supported civil rights. He tried to strengthen the act signed by Eisenhower. Kennedy sent another civil rights bill to Congress in June 1963. Churches and African American leaders **lobbied** Congress to pass the bill. Congress was still debating the bill when Kennedy was shot and killed in November 1963. Vice President Lyndon B. Johnson became the new president. Johnson promised to get the civil rights bill passed.

It took another eight months of debate before Congress agreed to make the *Civil Rights Act of 1964* a law. This law finally allowed the federal government to prevent many forms of racial discrimination.

President Johnson signed the *Civil Rights Act of 1964* on July 2 (left). The act banned segregation in public places. It also made it illegal to discriminate against someone based on their race, gender, or religion.

bill
: a requested new law that has not yet been passed

lobbied
: sought to influence

CASE STUDY

Freedom Summer

In the 1960s, about half the population in Mississippi were African American. However, no African American had been elected to state office in Mississippi since 1877. Unfair election practices and threats of violence stopped many African Americans from voting.

The Student Nonviolent Coordinating Committee (SNCC) held a Freedom Summer in June 1964 (above). The aim was to register as many African Americans as possible to vote. Volunteers flocked to Mississippi. Many were white American students from the North. During this summer, several civil rights activists were killed. Others were beaten and arrested. Churches and African American homes were bombed or burned. Still, more African Americans were registered to vote in Mississippi than ever before.

Divisions Within

1960s–1970s

The African American community was divided over the best way to end discrimination. Dr. Martin Luther King, Jr., believed that peaceful protest was the answer. Some other leaders supported different tactics. Several new protest groups emerged, and they challenged the nonviolent solution.

In 1966, an African American student named James Meredith led a march. He hoped to encourage more African Americans in Mississippi to vote. This march was known as the March Against Fear. The protest was peaceful, but many marchers were still arrested.

After the arrests, Stokely Carmichael took a different stand. He declared the need for "black power." He called for African Americans to have greater economic and political power. The Black Power movement encouraged African Americans to become independent.

Black Power inspired another group—the Black Panther Party. This party promoted civil rights and self-defense for African Americans. However, its willingness to use violence frightened many people.

Another major group was the Black Muslims. This group believed in economic and political independence. It believed that African Americans had a right to defend themselves with force. One of its leaders, Malcolm X, eventually encouraged more peaceful solutions. He was later killed for his beliefs.

Malcolm X (left) adopted the letter X as his last name. It represented the unknown name of his African ancestors. It was a symbol of protest against injustice.

These three medal winners at the 1968 Olympic Games wore Black Panther berets to show their support for the party. The gold medalist, Lee Evans, raised his fist in a Black Power gesture.

> **"Usually when people are sad they don't do anything. They just cry over their condition. But when they get angry, they bring about a change."**
>
> —*Malcolm X, 1965*

CASE STUDY

The 1968 Olympic Games

Some African American athletes protested during the 1968 Olympic Games in Mexico City. They wanted to call attention to civil rights conditions in the United States. Sprinters Tommie Smith and John Carlos won medals in the 200-meters. As they received their medals, Smith and Carlos raised their fists in the Black Power salute. They were sent home immediately as punishment by the United States Olympic Committee.

Later that week, four American runners finished in the lead of the 400 meters. Led by winner Lee Evans, the medal winners wore Black Panther berets on the awards platform. Lee raised his fist in salute. This time, the runners were not punished by the USOC.

Smith and Carlos's protest angered many people. The Olympic Games officials decided that the athletes' actions went against what the Olympics represented. Political protests were later banned in the Olympics.

Civil Rights Today

1968 Onwards

By the end of the 1960s, the Civil Rights Movement had suffered great blows. Both Dr. Martin Luther King, Jr., and Malcom X had been assassinated. There was **friction** within and between many civil rights groups. The movement had lost its key leaders, yet the great successes they had **achieved** lived on.

Many legal battles had been won. The NAACP had helped desegregate schools and other public places. Civil rights laws were being enforced. Also, workers rights had been improved through nonviolent protests. In time, new leaders emerged to continue the progress.

While discrimination is less widespread today, it still exists. Today, the focus for activist groups such as the NAACP has changed. They are no longer battling to end segregation or to win the right to vote. Instead they are fighting for equal jobs, education, and housing opportunities. Civil rights groups are trying to get more young people involved in politics too, so that they will have a voice in their own future. Much progress has been made, but the work of the Civil Rights Movement continues.

...UNTIL JUSTICE ROLLS DOWN LIKE WATERS
AND RIGHTEOUSNESS LIKE A MIGHTY STREAM

Many civil rights activists lost their lives during the struggle. The Civil Rights Memorial Center in Montgomery, Alabama, honors the memory of those who took part in the Civil Rights Movement (left).

Dr. King and his wife, Coretta Scott King, traveled around the country in order to spread the message of civil rights through nonviolence. Mrs. King traveled and spoke about her husband and civil rights up until her death in 2006.

friction
disagreement between people

achieved
done; completed

constantly
without stopping

PROFILE

Coretta Scott King 1927–2006

Coretta Scott King was the wife of Dr. Martin Luther King, Jr. She attended his marches, speeches, and ceremonies. Coretta Scott King **constantly** worked to raise support for the Civil Rights Movement. She was called the "First Lady of Civil Rights."

After Dr. King's death, Mrs. King continued to fight for his dream of equal rights for all. In 1968, she founded the King Center. This center was established to promote equality through nonviolence. In 1969, she established the Coretta Scott King Book Award. Because of her efforts, the entire country recognizes Dr. King's birthday, January 15, as a national holiday.

The Movement

The journey African Americans made from slavery to freedom was long and painful. Hatred and violence threatened to stop the Civil Rights Movement. Fortunately, justice finally won out. Civil Rights: The Movement looks at some of the key events and leaders that shaped the Civil Rights Movement of the 1960s.

1. Using Civil Rights: The Movement as a reference, describe the issues and impact of *Brown v. Board of Education*.

2. When and where did Dr. Martin Luther King, Jr., give his famous "I have a dream" speech?

3. Martin Luther King, Jr. believed that the government should treat everyone fairly.
   - How was King's approach to civil rights different from those of other protest groups? How was it similar?
   - If you were being treated unfairly, how would you respond? How does this help you understand what you've read?

Asesoras

Sally Creel, Ed.D.
Asesora de currículo

Leann Iacuone, M.A.T., NBCT, ATC
Riverside Unified School District

Jill Tobin
Semifinalista
Maestro del año de California
Burbank Unified School District

Créditos de imágenes: pág.2 Robert Matton AB/Alamy; pág.5 Zoonar GmbH/Alamy; pág.13 Hillary Dunlap; pág.14 Amiko Kauderer/NASA; pág.18 Glenn Research Center/NASA; pág.19 iStock; págs.20–21 (ilustraciones) Chris Sabatino; todas las demás imágenes cortesía de Shutterstock.

Teacher Created Materials
5301 Oceanus Drive
Huntington Beach, CA 92649-1030
http://www.tcmpub.com

ISBN 978-1-4258-4653-4

La Tierra y la luna

Torrey Maloof

To be a poor man is hard, but to be a poor race in a land of dollars is the very bottom of hardships.

—W.E.B. Du Bois, educator and author

CIVIL RIGHTS

Early Struggles

Civil rights activists wanted equal treatment for African Americans. They worked to overturn the laws that allowed African Americans and other groups to be treated poorly because of their race. This difficult struggle lasted many years.

Civil Rights: Early Struggles looks at the situation facing African Americans in the United States after slavery ended in 1865. It examines unjust laws, and it looks at some of the key people who prepared the nation for the Civil Rights Movement.

CONTENTS

Rights Denied

1865–1875

In 1866, African Americans had good reason to dream of a brighter future. The American Civil War had ended the year before. The defeated Confederate states in the South had lost their battle with the North. All slaves were now free. The central government had also started a program to rebuild the South.

African Americans were slowly gaining some rights. The Fifteenth Amendment to the Constitution (1870) gave men of all races the right to vote. Then the *Civil Rights Act of 1875* guaranteed everyone equal **access** to public places. However, many states, particularly in the South, refused to take notice of these laws. They made their own laws that **discriminated** against African Americans. There was also a serious problem with hate groups who would **terrorize** African Americans. The dream of equal rights seemed to be slipping away.

Jim Crow laws created separate services for whites and African Americans (left).

Civil Rights Time Line

April 9, 1865	The Civil War ends. U.S. President Abraham Lincoln frees all slaves.
April 9, 1866	The *Civil Rights Act of 1866* is passed, protecting the rights of former slaves.
February 3, 1870	The 15th Amendment to the Constitution is officially approved.
March 1, 1875	The *Civil Rights Act of 1875* is passed to stop discrimination in public places.
1883	The U.S. Supreme Court rules against the *Civil Rights Act of 1875*.
May 18, 1896	In *Plessy v. Ferguson*, the U.S. Supreme Court rules that "separate but equal" services do not violate the Constitution.
1909	The National Association for the Advancement of Colored Peoples (NAACP) is formed.
June 21, 1915	The Supreme Court outlaws "grandfather clauses" in *Guinn v. United States.*
June 25, 1941	The Fair Employment Practices Commission is set up.
1942	The first chapter of the Congress of Racial Equality (CORE) forms.
July 26, 1948	President Harry Truman orders an end to segregation in the military.
1954	The *Brown v. Board of Education* case ends legal separation of African Americans and whites in public schools.
December 1, 1955	Rosa Parks refuses to give up her seat on a Montgomery bus. Her arrest sparks the Montgomery Bus Boycott.
September 1957	Federal troops are sent to protect African American students in Little Rock, Arkansas.
August 28, 1963	About 250,000 people attend the March on Washington.
July 2, 1964	The *Civil Rights Act of 1964* is signed into law.
August 6, 1965	The *Voting Act of 1965* is signed. The act outlaws unfair voting practices.
April 4, 1968	Dr. Martin Luther King, Jr., is shot and killed in Memphis, Tennessee.

access
the ability or right to enter

discriminated
treated unfairly because of race, age, or disability

terrorize
threaten with violence

Jim Crow Laws

1875–1965

Slavery ended in 1865. All African American men won the right to vote in 1870. Even so, there were still problems for African Americans in some states. Many states ignored the central government's call to treat African Americans as equals. Some whites continued to view and treat these U.S. citizens as **inferior** to themselves.

In 1877, President Rutherford B. Hayes withdrew central government troops from the Southern states. The troops had been protecting African Americans' rights since the Civil War ended. After the troops left, these states began introducing **segregation** laws.

These laws—called Jim Crow laws—allowed businesses and governments to keep African Americans and whites separated. The states claimed their laws provided "separate but equal" services. This was not the case, however. Services for whites were usually much better.

The U.S. Constitution allowed individual states to decide how they would run their own voting processes and their own schools. Southern states used this right to enforce many discriminatory laws.

The resources provided to African American schools, such as this school in Virginia (left), were far from equal to those given to most white schools.

This man is buying theater tickets in 1935. Segregation laws meant that there were separate ticket counters and entrances for African Americans.

inferior
of low rank or importance

segregation
the separation of people because of their race

U.S. Supreme Court
the highest court in the United States

CASE STUDY

Plessy v. Ferguson

Louisiana introduced a law in 1890 that required separate accommodation on trains for African Americans. A group of civil-rights activists from New Orleans believed this violated, or broke the law of, the Constitution. They wanted to test it in the courts. In 1892, they had a man named Homer Plessy purchase a first-class train ticket. Plessy then boarded a "white carriage." The train conductor arrested Plessy because he was part African American.

Louisiana Judge John Ferguson found Plessy guilty of breaking the law. The case went all the way to the **U.S. Supreme Court** (above, right). In 1896, the Supreme Court ruled in favor of the state of Louisiana. It said "separate but equal" services did not violate the Constitution. This decision allowed Jim Crow laws to continue in the South.

Early Leaders

1880s–1918

Two key civil rights leaders **emerged** in the late 1800s. Both sought the rights promised to African Americans after the Civil War. However, their ideas about how to gain those rights differed.

Booker T. Washington was born a slave. He grew up to be a teacher and **reformer**. Washington did not focus on fighting directly for rights. Instead, he focused on education and jobs. Washington believed that **economic** power for African Americans would gradually result in more rights.

W.E.B. Du Bois was also a teacher and reformer. He did not agree with Washington. Du Bois focused on fighting for equal rights immediately. Du Bois urged for protest and direct action. In 1909, Du Bois helped found the NAACP. This group was dedicated to seeking rights for African Americans and others.

Booker T. Washington (right) was principal of the Tuskegee Institute in Alabama for 33 years.

W.E.B Du Bois, the first African American to earn a doctorate degree from Harvard University, taught at Atlanta University.

Below is the office of the NAACP's magazine, *The Crisis.* W.E.B. Du Bois ran the magazine for 25 years.

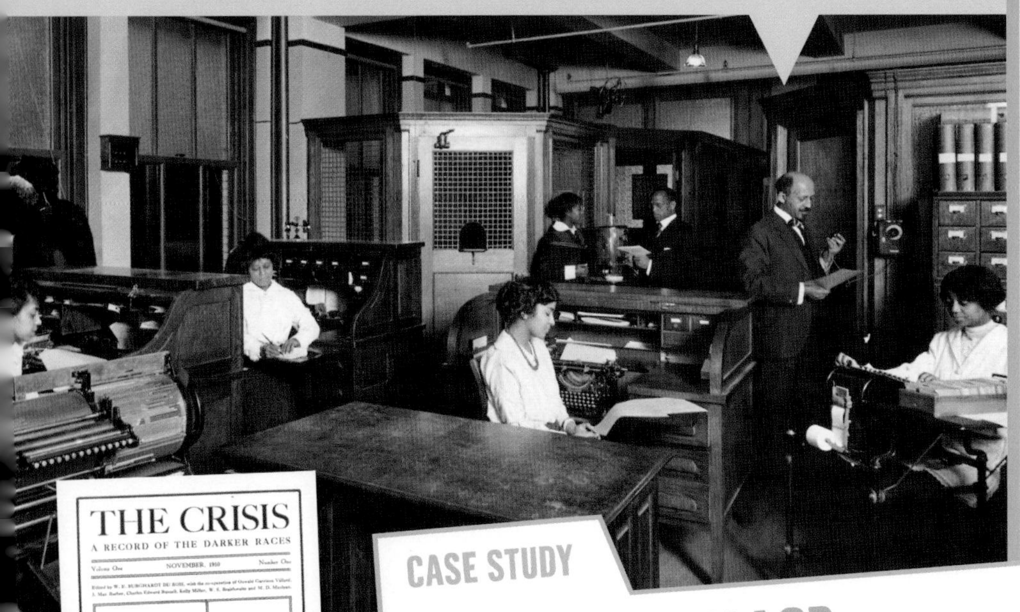

The NAACP started publishing the magazine *The Crisis* in 1910 (above, inset). It was a voice for civil rights.

emerged
became known; came into view

reformer
a person who works for positive change

economic
relating to finances and money

CASE STUDY

Founding the NAACP

In 1909, a group consisting of both whites and African Americans formed the NAACP. Members of the organization, including W.E.B. Du Bois, worked to improve the legal and civil rights of African Americans across the country. During its early years, the NAACP fought especially hard to end hate crimes and to guarantee fair trials for people accused of crimes.

In 1918, the NAACP succeeded in convincing President Woodrow Wilson to publicly speak out against hate crimes and against people taking the law into their own hands.

Defending Their Country

1914–1948

More than 350,000 African Americans served in the U.S. military during World War I (1914–1918). They wanted to fight, but most ended up in support roles. African American soldiers were made to serve in their own segregated units.

During World War II (1938–1945), more than one million African Americans joined the U.S. forces. As in World War I, African American soldiers mainly served in separate African American units. However, by the end of the war, several units began to desegregate. In 1948, President Truman ordered the permanent desegregation of the U.S. armed forces.

Despite discrimination, African Americans fought bravely during World War II. Benjamin O. Davis, Jr., became the first black lieutenant general in the Air Force. In addition, Dorie Miller received the Navy Cross medal for his bravery at Pearl Harbor. Back home, though, African Americans still had many battles to win.

The first African American pilot crew was formed in Tuskegee, Alabama, in 1941. The "Tuskegee Airmen" became one of the most respected fighter groups in World War II. The success of African American troops had a larger impact, too. President Harry Truman ordered the end of segregation in the military in July 1948.

During World War II, many African Americans moved North to work in the defense industries. Some whites in the North feared that African Americans might take their jobs away from them. This led to dozens of riots between African Americans and whites in 1943 (above). Some 800 people were injured in the violence.

> **"Winning democracy for the [African American] is winning the war for democracy!"**
>
> *—Labor leader A. Philip Randolph, quoted in a March on Washington flyer, 1941*

CASE STUDY

The "Double V" Campaign

African American soldiers in World War II were fighting against a racist German government. Yet some African Americans back home could not even vote. In February 1942, the *Pittsburgh Courier* newspaper launched a "Double V" campaign. It demanded that African American soldiers be given full voting and other citizenship rights.

Double V stood for victory over Germany in the war—and victory over racism in the United States. The campaign was soon promoted nationwide. It kept the issue of the unequal treatment of African Americans in the public eye.

NAACP vs Jim Crow

1909–1954

The NAACP decided to fight in court against the unfair treatment of African Americans. It took a case against "grandfather clauses" to the U.S. Supreme Court. The unfair clauses allowed white men who were not able to read to still vote. The laws said people did not need to take a literacy test to vote if they had a grandfather who voted before 1866. Since African Americans only won the right to vote in 1870, the clause could never apply to them. In 1915, the U.S. Supreme Court ruled that "grandfather clauses" discriminated against African Americans.

Between 1880 and 1930, more than 3,000 African Americans were killed by mobs. The NAACP worked hard to try and get the central government to make laws that stopped the violence. The NAACP was unsuccessful in getting such laws passed. Luckily, its exposure of the violence helped to greatly reduce the number of attacks by 1940.

These and other challenges began to have an effect on Jim Crow laws. The greatest victories for the NAACP came when it began to focus on the unequal segregation of public schools in the 1930s.

Louisiana banned African Americans from living in neighborhoods where most homes were owned by whites. The NAACP successfully fought against this law in 1916.

A group of African American women sit outside their home in Monroe, Louisiana, 1906 (left).

The U.S. Supreme Court forced the University of Oklahoma to accept African American student George McLaurin in 1948. The university made McLaurin sit apart from other students (above, right).

> **"There is in this world no such force as the force of a man [or woman] determined to rise. The human soul cannot be permanently chained."**
>
> *—NAACP leader W.E.B. Du Bois, March 5, 1910*

PROFILE

Thurgood Marshall 1908–1993

The NAACP picked African American lawyer Thurgood Marshall (right) to lead its legal team in 1936. It was a very good decision. Marshall challenged the Jim Crow laws that created separate public schools for African American and white students. He also argued for equal pay for African American teachers in Maryland and Virginia.

His most famous victory came in 1954 with the case of *Brown v. Board of Education*. Marshall successfully argued to end the segregation of schools in the United States. Marshall won 29 out of the 32 cases he brought before the U.S. Supreme Court. In 1967, Marshall became the first African American to be chosen to serve on the Supreme Court.

Nonviolent Protest

1942–1961

Some civil rights activists felt that progress to end segregation was too slow. The NAACP had won some important cases, but discrimination was still widespread. These activists planned to oppose racial violence with nonviolent protests. These nonviolent protests included marches and "sit-ins." For example, many protestors sat peacefully in segregated restaurants until they were served or arrested. Up to 70,000 students joined these sit-ins across the South.

James Farmer helped found the Congress of Racial Equality (CORE) in April 1942. CORE was inspired by the Indian peace activist Mohandas Gandhi. A CORE activist named James Lawson developed a set of rules to be used at sit-ins. Protestors were not to strike back if cursed or attacked. They were asked to be courteous and friendly at all times.

The Student Nonviolent Coordinating Committee (SNCC) formed in 1960. SNCC worked to register African Americans to vote. Members of these groups often risked their lives working for social change in the South. They would have a big influence on the nationwide fight for civil rights in the 1960s.

This sit-in against segregated lunch counters took place in Charlotte, North Carolina (right).

Dr. Martin Luther King, Jr., founded the Southern Christian Leadership Conference (SCLC) in 1957. King wanted to attract national attention to racial inequality in the South. Here King and other SCLC members are protesting about poor education and housing for African Americans in Boston, Massachusetts, in 1965.

> **"You don't have to ride Jim Crow! On June the third the high court said, when you ride interstate, Jim Crow is dead..."**
>
> —*Lyrics from the song "You Don't Have to Ride Jim Crow," by CORE activists Bayard Rustin and George Houser, 1947*

CASE STUDY

Journey of Reconciliation

In 1946, the U.S. Supreme Court ruled that segregated public transportation between states was illegal. A group of CORE activists decided to test this ruling. They bought bus and train tickets from Washington, D.C. to Kentucky in April 1947. The African American and white American activists sat side-by-side. They were arrested many times on their journey for breaking Jim Crow laws.

This "Journey of Reconciliation" inspired others. Minister Fred Shuttlesworth led a protest against bus segregation in 1956 (above, right).

Montgomery Bus Boycott

1955–1956

Most bus passengers in the late 1950s were African Americans. However, they were not allowed to sit in the front rows of the bus. Those seats were reserved for white passengers. African Americans entered the bus to pay their fare, and then left the bus. They then re-entered from the doors at the back of the bus. An African American passenger was not allowed to share a row with a white passenger. African Americans were also required to give up their seats for white passengers if the front was full.

On December 1, 1955, local NAACP member Rosa Parks was arrested in Montgomery, Alabama. She had refused to give her seat on a bus to a white man. African American leaders encouraged all African Americans to stop using the city's buses in protest. Many went to work in taxis or cars. Others walked for miles. The city's bus companies and downtown businesses lost a lot of money.

In November 1956, the U.S. Supreme Court banned segregation on buses. State laws soon changed to allow African Americans to sit anywhere in buses. The successful boycott ended soon after. It had lasted 381 days.

Most of the city's African Americans supported the Montgomery Bus Boycott (left). Some white citizens supported the boycott as well. The bus system lost about 70 percent of its regular passengers.

Rosa Parks was arrested for refusing to give up her seat on a bus. This was the event that prompted the Montgomery Bus Boycott. Former NAACP leader E.D. Nixon used Parks' case to challenge the Montgomery bus segregation law.

> **"People always say that I didn't give up my seat because I was tired, but that isn't true. I was not tired physically, or no more tired that I usually was at the end of a working day… No, the only tired I was, was tired of giving in."**
>
> —*Rosa Parks, 1992*

PROFILE

Rosa Parks 1913–2005

Rosa Parks had a long history of fighting for civil rights. In 1943, she became the first woman to join the local NAACP chapter. She served as secretary of the organization. In the summer of 1955, she attended a class in Tennessee that taught people how to organize movements for social change.

Rosa Parks moved with her family to Detroit in 1957. She continued her civil rights work. She was awarded the Presidential Medal of Freedom in 1996. In 1999, she was awarded the Congressional Gold Medal. Rosa Parks became a hero of the Civil Rights Movement.

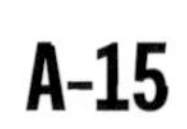

Early Struggles

The journey African Americans made from slavery to freedom was long and painful. Hatred and violence threatened to stop the Civil Rights Movement. Fortunately, justice finally won out. Civil Rights: Early Struggles looks at the unfair laws that stripped African Americans of their rights, and at the early efforts of activists who sought to overturn these laws.

1. Using Civil Rights: Early Struggles as a reference, describe the impact of Jim Crow Laws on African Americans. What court decision supported states that enforced these laws?

2. African American soldiers won praise for their skills and bravery in World War I and World War II. What was the name of the campaign to get these soldiers full U.S. citizenship rights?

3. Civil rights activists in the 1940s started using nonviolent protests to draw attention to discrimination. These peaceful activists did not strike back even when they were attacked.
   - Do you think nonviolent actions are more effective than violence? Why or why not?
   - What sorts of issues do people protest peacefully about today?

Contenido

Nuestro hogar

Todos vivimos en la Tierra. La Tierra es un **planeta** redondo en el espacio que **rota**, o gira. También se desplaza alrededor de una gran estrella brillante llamada el sol.

La Tierra siempre se está moviendo.

5

Día y noche

No puedes sentirlo, pero la Tierra siempre está en movimiento. Tarda 24 horas en dar un giro completo.

Es de día en Nueva York.

Mientras rota, la parte de la Tierra de frente al sol recibe luz y calor. En esa parte del planeta es de día.

La Tierra rota sobre su eje, como un trompo.

Los ejes de la Tierra

La Tierra rota sobre su **eje**. Un eje es una línea imaginaria alrededor de la cual gira la Tierra.

Al mismo tiempo, la otra parte de la Tierra está oculta del sol. En esa parte de la Tierra es de noche.

Es de día en un lado de la Tierra.
Es de noche al otro lado de la Tierra.

Mientras la Tierra rota, la noche se convierte en día y el día se convierte en noche.

Por la mañana, parece que el sol sale. Sale por el este. El sol alcanza su punto más alto en la tarde.

Al atardecer, el sol parece ocultarse en el cielo. Se pone por el oeste.

Buenas noches, luna

Cuando el sol se pone, es más fácil ver la luna en el cielo. No siempre tiene el mismo aspecto. ¡Cambia todas las noches!

Día o noche

Principalmente vemos la luna de noche. Pero algunas veces podemos verla durante el día.

La luna cambia porque se mueve alrededor de la Tierra. Estos cambios se llaman **fases**.

Esto muestra las fases de la luna.

El sol ilumina la mitad de la luna, tal como ilumina la Tierra. La otra mitad de la luna está en la oscuridad.

Aquí solamente podemos ver parte del lado iluminado de la luna.

A medida que la luna se mueve alrededor de la Tierra, vemos parte del lado iluminado.

Caminata lunar

Solamente 12 personas han caminado sobre la luna.

Como una vez al mes, todo el lado de la luna iluminado por el sol está frente a la Tierra. Esta fase se llama **luna llena**.

Cuando la parte iluminada por el sol está oculta de la Tierra, no podemos ver la luna. Esta fase se llama **luna nueva**.

Cuando hay luna nueva, parece que la luna no está en el cielo.

luna nueva

¡En marcha!

La Tierra está en constante movimiento. ¡Y la luna también! A causa de todo este movimiento, tenemos días y noches. Tenemos diferentes fases de la luna. Y tenemos un lugar especial al que llamamos *hogar*.

Así es como se ve la Tierra desde la luna.

¡Hagamos ciencia!

¿Por qué a veces la luna tiene diferentes aspectos? ¡Intenta esto y verás!

Qué conseguir

- lámpara
- papel y lápiz
- pelota

Qué hacer

1. Supón que la pelota es la luna, tu cabeza es la Tierra y la lámpara es el sol. Coloca la lámpara en el medio de la habitación con todas las otras luces apagadas.

2. Sostén la pelota y muévela al frente de la luz.

3. Gírala toda lentamente. Observa las sombras sobre la pelota. Son como las sombras en la luna.

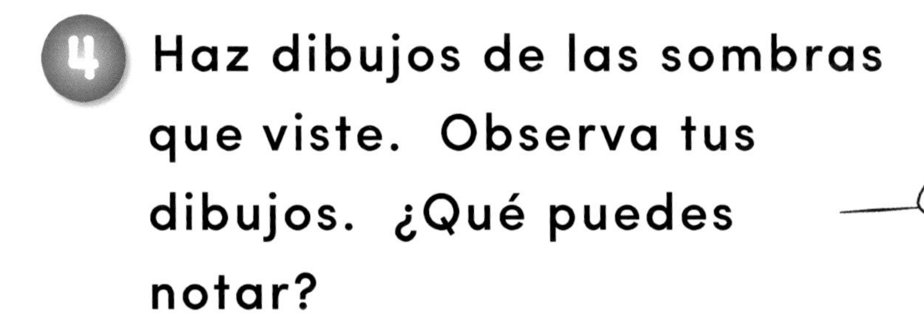

4. Haz dibujos de las sombras que viste. Observa tus dibujos. ¿Qué puedes notar?

Glosario

eje: la línea imaginaria alrededor de la cual gira la Tierra

fases: las ocho figuras del lado iluminado de la luna

luna llena: la luna cuando luce como un círculo brillante y completo

luna nueva: la luna cuando está completamente oscura

planeta: un objeto grande y redondo en el espacio que se mueve alrededor de una estrella

rota: gira o da vueltas

Índice

¡Tu turno!

Fases de la luna

Observa la luna todos los días. Dibuja su forma. Observa cómo cambia. ¿Cuántas fases puedes ver?